Buster B. Bluecrab

Written & Illustrated by
Glenn Linton

This book is dedicated to Charlotte Collins,
the student who taught me that you are never too old
to follow your dreams.
She fed my confidence and gave me inspiration.
I will always be grateful to her
and thankful to have known her.

ISBN 0-9763360-8-1

Printed in the United States of America.
First Printing, 2004

Library of Congress Catalog Number 2004116835

Oh, oh, o-o-o-o-o—that tickles! A crab net is brushing my stomach. Suddenly I am whisked through the water. I'm scared as string surrounds me like a spider web. I suddenly explode out of the salt water and am grabbed by gloved hands as human eyes examine my fins. Now I am somersaulting into a bushel basket that is sitting in an inner tube. As I try to crawl into a dark corner, I am showered with pine needles. I know the sun will quickly kill me.

The last few minutes have been horrible—like time standing still. I'm caught in a motionless frame and I see my whole life flash before me.

Oh—by the way, I'm Buster B. Bluecrab. (Later I'll explain why they call me Buster.) Until a few minutes ago, I lived in the Chesapeake Bay. My favorite part of the bay is the waters surrounding the Eastern Shore. I *love* the Eastern Shore. Here the water is so-o-o-o-o clean and salty. Not all water is clean! In fact, some of the creeks and rivers are downright murky—na-a-a-a-sty! Would you want to live in a dirty house? My house is the Chesapeake Bay, and it is a very, very large home. I share my bay home with other marine life: fish, turtles, eels, oysters, clams, and all kinds of other underwater life.

For the last decade, people like you have been cleaning my bay by taking trash and pollutants out of my waters. By trash, I mean cans, plastics, and paper. There are also types of trash that you cannot see. They are invisible poisons—pollutants that have suffocated the bay's vegetation. Yes, we have plants growing on the sandy, muddy bottom, just like farmers grow in their fields. Someday the Chesapeake Bay will be so-o-o-o-o good for me. I'll be able to hide anywhere!

Why would Ole Buster want to hide? Protection! Hiding is how I protect myself. When I was just a young crab, there was seaweed—tall, dark, slimy grass—everywhere! Then people, factories, and solid waste killed it in most places. Now parts of my home are a barren underwater desert.

But there's still *some* seaweed, and I was hiding out in it when some kid scooped me out of my paradise and dumped me in a bushel basket.

• • •

Matthew looks down at the crab he netted and wonders whether it's a peeler. His dad told him that if he isn't sure whether a crab is a peeler, he should keep it anyway—it might mean a dollar in his pocket.

I'm looking through the pine needles, nice and comfy in my dark spot in the basket. This capture is a ritual that has happened to me many times. I'm not a peeler. A peeler is a crab that's about to shed its shell, and I'm not. Every time a crab loses its shell, it gets bigger and bigger—that's how a crab grows!

Why is Ole Buster B. Bluecrab worth so much money when he's in the peeler stage? Because then he becomes very soft—cotton-ball soft. And after he sheds his shell, he could become a soft crab sandwich!

Matthew takes his bushel basket out of the inner tube and hands it up, up, up toward hands reaching from the dock.

"Boy, this is heavy," shouts Brooks, the owner of the crab house. He carries the basket toward a crab float where water is being forced down into a vat full of crabs to create oxygen so the crabs can breathe.

"Hey, Johnny, come over here and help me count these peelers that Matthew just handed me," Brooks calls. Johnny walks over to the basket and reaches into it; he raises a peeler to eye level and glares at the fin. (The redder the fin, the ranker the crab, and the sooner it will shed.)

He counts, "One." Brooks calls, "Two." This crab goes into one vat, that crab goes into another vat, depending on how red the fin appears.

"Three . . ." There's total concentration on each splash. ". . . eight," the culler yells. "Twenty-one."

Occasionally Johnny or Brooks drops a crab between the floats and the dock, but they are just as careful with these crabs as they are with the ones they throw in the vats.

4

"Twenty-eight." These crabs are not peelers—not right now. "Forty-two." But one day they *will* become peelers. "Fifty-five."

A gloved hand reaches down and wraps around me. My fin shoots up and I'm released, falling, falling. Down, down, down I go, hearing "Sixty-one" just before I splash into the cool water. I dash for a pole.

I wait! I listen! Wait some more! Listen some more! Then I peek around the pole, expecting to be snatched again, but no one seems to care about me.

I hear "Seventy-two" echoing off the water. My alarm-guard oo-o-o-o-zes out of my shell. I start to relax. I look toward the distant waters for seaweed, but I am not concerned. Fish do not want me—not now.

My shell is hard—like an old football. My nerves begin to calm down, and soon they're as calm as the shallow water above the sandy bottom where I'm hiding.

But listen! Wait! I start to dash across the sand, cautiously at first. Then I zoom as dust flows up behind my tracks. It looks like I move on steam as I dart toward some seaweed in the distant waters.

As I move, I see a big brown trout zoo-o-o-ooming in on my smokey trail. His radar detects me, but I'm not worried. It's nice to be "hard-headed" once in a while! I reach the edge of the nice slimy grass as the fish veers off like a fighter jet leaving its formation.

As I enter the dark, grassy forest, I get the same feeling an ant gets when he crawls through a lawn. Deeper and darker the forest becomes. If you were looking for Ole Buster, the only thing you'd see would be the reflections off my glasses.

I sneak around for days. I'm here one minute, there the next. I snatch a piece of minnow now and then or even old flakes of fin from another unfortunate crab.

My claws carry things: food, shells, wood; they also help to protect me. Most people think I eat with the teeth along the ends of my claws, but guess what? I have a mouth just like you do. I eat the same way you do. My food is raw, not cooked, but it *is* salted like some of your foods.

Ole B. Likes to lie low and hide in the summer because everyone is trying to catch me! People like you, your grandma and grandpa, your dad and mom, your sisters and brothers . . . and Matthew!

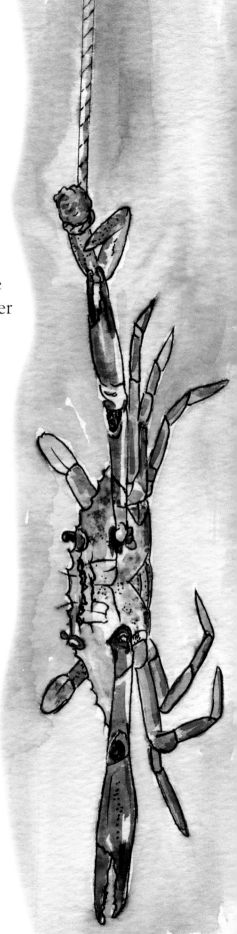

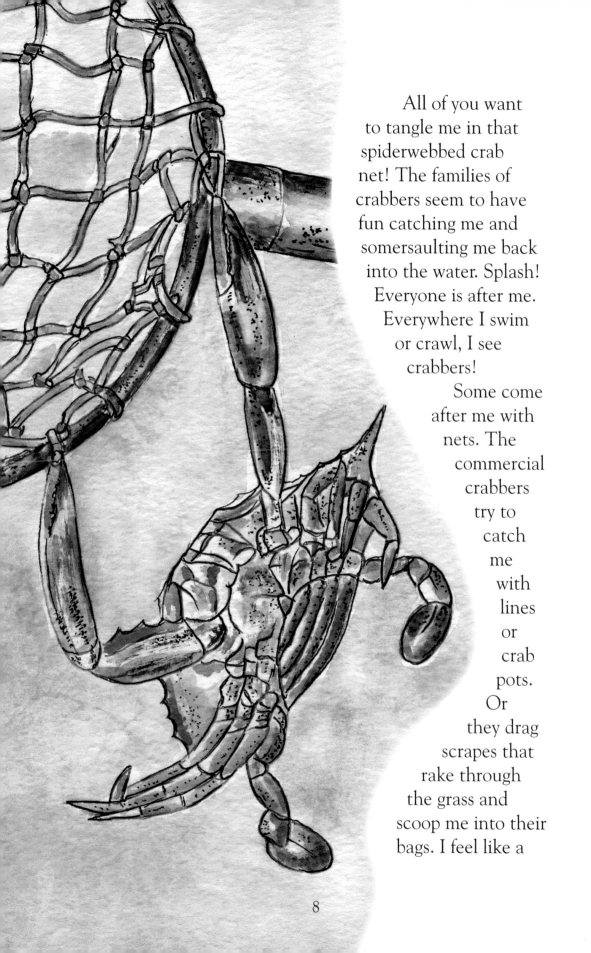

All of you want to tangle me in that spiderwebbed crab net! The families of crabbers seem to have fun catching me and somersaulting me back into the water. Splash! Everyone is after me. Everywhere I swim or crawl, I see crabbers!

Some come after me with nets. The commercial crabbers try to catch me with lines or crab pots. Or they drag scrapes that rake through the grass and scoop me into their bags. I feel like a

fugitive who's innocent—I didn't rob a bank, but everyone's after me any way!

The hardest temptation for me to resist is a baited crab pot. Oh—that wonderful smell of fish oil drives me cra-a-a-azy! It's just like the garlic smell of a pizza or spaghetti that drifts up, up, up your nose when you pass an Italian restaurant. That delightful oil coming from a crab pot drives all crabs crazy.

I approach a pot, looking through the wire mesh. I see all kinds of captured crabs—sooks, peelers, and jimmies (hard crabs). They just can't resist that aroma of fish oil! They look sad, like puppies in a cage.

Suddenly, the pot shoots up in the air, leaving a trail of bubbles. I just stare, dazed. A minute later the wire box floats down to the muddy bottom . . . EMPTY!

I crawl for a while, saddened by the loss of my fine finned friends and remembering the great times we've had together.

9

My claws droop as I crawl aimlessly toward nowhere. I don't know how many hours or days pass. Time is not a problem; we have no clocks or watches down on the bottom. We measure time only by survival.

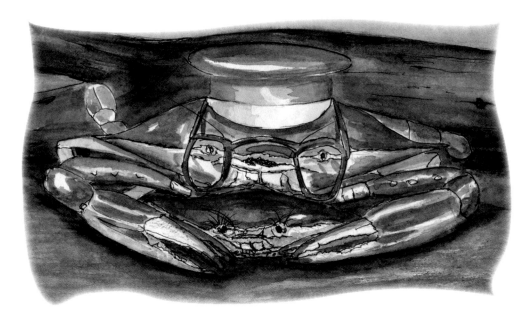

Suddenly, I see Pammy, and I come to life again.
I have protected Pammy every time she has started to
shed. You see, Pammy is a female—a woman—you might
call her a *sook*. When she sheds, she becomes a very,
very, ver-r-r-ry soft crab and needs protection. Fish *love* a
soft crab!

When Pammy is in the soft stage, she connects
underneath me, and they call us a *doubler*. This happens
more often during a full moon. Later, Pammy will become
hard again, and she'll know instinctively when it's time
to detach from me. How fast she hardens depends on the
water temperature. The warmer the water, the quicker she
will become hard again.

Soon Pammy will be old enough to start producing tiny
orange eggs under her apron. When she does this, she'll be
called a *sponge* crab because the 5,000 or so eggs under her
look and feel like a sponge. Many, many eggs do not make it
to the crab stage; fish like them for lunch, eels like them for
breakfast, and even other crabs like to eat them. They're a
tasty delicacy for any roaming marine life.

Pammy and I stay near each other for a day, basking in the mud and talking about old times. Then I wander off into deeper water, seeing a relative here, a pot there as I sink into deeper, darker, and colder water. As I go deeper, I feel the current getting stronger.

Current in the water is like wind blowing on the land. The water moves swiftly as I swim deeper and deeper. I start to see sparkles from the tops of my eyes. In the distance above me, I see water twisting and turning, I instinctively turn my fins like the propeller of an outboard motor.

I zoom down, deeper, deeper, until I'm buried in the mud.

The flashes are coming closer together and more often. The drumming noise is getting louder and louder. I peek through the mud with one eye upward. I see bolts of fire bounce off the surface of the water. As they hit, they seem to light up the marine bottom like a camera flash shooting off.

The storm is directly above me! The flashes are stronger and stronger! The thunder is louder and louder! I just want to bury deeper and deeper in the mud, but I can't because I've drilled down to a rock-hard surface.

After a while the storm moves off in the distance. The lights and noise fade away.

The current slows to almost a halt. I begin to dig myself out of the mud and rise to the surface of the muddy bottom.

It is frig-g-g-gid here! I begin to slither up the muddy hills into the warmer and brighter water. As I rise, the water warms me and makes me feel like I just showered—fresh! Oh, what a wonderful feeling.

I level off in four feet of water. Just ahead is eelgrass—seaweed. I float down into the dark grass for a safe nap. I snuggle in the weeds. The only way you can tell I'm there are the bubbles floating to the surface every once in a while. It seems like I'll have hours and hours and hours of heavenly sleep.

But then, I hear bouncing, bumping, and dragging sounds on the surface of the bottom. The sounds are getting closer and closer.

Oh, no—it's a scrape! I listen for a few more seconds before I peek over the seaweed. It looks like a twister coming toward me. Grass and filmy mud fly everywhere. If I don't want to get caught, I'd better move out of the way of this giant rake combing the weeds.

I dart to the left as a piece of the metal bar comes near me. I barely escape as the rake creates a holocaust—

destroying everything in its path—just like a rolling tornado!

I lie low and do not move for a few minutes. I am still trembling from the thought of the destruction I have just avoided. When I'm nervous, bubbles fly everywhere, and this crisis is no exception.

The crabber makes circles with his dredge, and I know it will be coming through the grass again. It reminds me of a farmer plowing a field or someone cutting grass. I start to move toward the barren desert, where no seaweed grows. I know there's no reason for the crabber to dredge there.

As I move through the seaweed toward the sand, my apron starts to loosen. Oh, no—this is a bad sign—I am shedding! My shell starts to lift from the apron. I'm now a *buster* crab. This is where I got my name. I've shed so many times that everyone started calling me Buster!

Everyone will want me now. I have to hide when I shed, and there's no one around to protect me like there is for Pammy.

I have to hide, but where? The more I shed, the weaker I become. I try to move, but it seems like

slo-o-o-ow motion compared to my traveling speed a few hours ago.

I've got to find a hiding place—a pole, a tire, a log, a branch—anything that will hide me from hungry fish.

My pace is slowing and slowing. I feel like I am dragging an anchor. My eyes dart from here to there. There to here. I look for a place to hide. Soon—very soon—I must find shelter. I *must* hide!

The water is becoming very shallow. The tide is falling. I am in less than a foot of water. My shell is breaking apart.

Oh—what can I do? No poles, no tires, no logs—I don't see one hiding place! The tide is falling—the water is only six inches deep. And I'm about to lose my shell!

I'm feeling very weak—almost limp. The water's only three inches deep. I start to slide. No—no! Don't let this be the end.

Down, down, down into a muddy hole I dig. Buried! Buried! I'm hidden in this slimy, dark hole, and the only evidence of my presence is the skeleton shell left in my tracks. I'm just lying here paralyzed. It will be a couple of hours before I can move. I just hope no one is crabbing in this area. They shouldn't be looking here—no seaweed, tires, trash, or poles. If only I could hide that shell!

• • •

"How many crabs have we caught today?" asks Katie.

Dustin looks in her direction and answers, "About twenty-three!"

"Dustin, Dustin—come over this way. There's nothing but sand and mud over there," Katie yells.

"Katie, I see an empty shell over here!" Dustin replies.

"Dus-s-s-tin, come over here right now!"

"Katie!"

"Dustin, I'm telling Mom."

"Al-l-l right," Dustin grumbles.

My eyes shoot straight into this boy's eyes. This is the end! He's still walking toward me. He's sixteen feet away and moving in my direction. Ten feet away. My shell is getting firmer, but I cannot move at all.

Seven feet!

"Dus-s-s-tin, come over here right now!"

Six feet!

"Dustin, I'm telling Mom!"

Four feet. I shut my eyes. I know he must be able to see the mud moving up and down, up and down with the beating of my heart!

Three feet. His shadow falls over me. I'm so nervous that the ground feels like a California earthquake. I'm shaking!

"Al-l-l right!" Dustin turns around as if he has not seen a thing. He walks away.

• • •

My shell has finally hardened. The water starts to rise, and within an hour, my hiding hole is overflowing. I can move a little, but my skin is still paper-shell soft. It's not until the tide has risen two feet that I'm able to move faster than a staggering crawl. I'd still be a great lunch for a fish!

It will be two more hours before I'm too hard for a fish to eat. I have to find another place to hide. Then it hits me—there are no crab dredgers around. I swim slowly and dizzily toward the dark grass.

Just before I start to dive into the grass jungle, I see a school of fish moving through the water above me. This has been a ver-r-r-y lucky day for me, I think as I touch the slimy weeds. I feel exhausted as I doze in the comfy bed I've made for myself. This will be a good night's sleep.

• • •

After a few days, I feel like new, but fatter and bigger than before. I've grown almost an inch after that last shedding.

The days are getting shorter and the nights cooler. The water temperature is dropping, leaves are falling, and butterflies are coloring the sky. The signs of fall are here.

I start to yawn. In the last few days, the water has cleared. No minnows, trout, or croaker anywhere. Rockfish are schooling and bunches are swimming over me. I can see more and more rockfish each passing day. Temperatures are dropping. Crab pots are gone! I am getting sleepy.

I head for deeper water. Darker water! Muddy water! I sink down deeper and look for more dark and muddy water. I drop down, down, down into a muddy bottom. I start to

bury myself in the mud. I'm yawning. Soon I'll settle down to hibernate—just like a bear!

I bury myself deeper in the mud. Yaw-aw-aw-n. The mud gushes around me. Down . . . down . . . dark . . . pitch black. I burrow down in the mud until I hit a rocky bottom.

I snooze. Peaceful dreams come quickly. Sleep, sleep, dream, drea-a-a-a-m, se-e-e-e-ee yo-o-o-ou al-l-l-l nex-x-x-xt sum-m-m-m-mer.

THE END

Crabby Facts

apron A crab's abdomen

bucky crab A crab that has shed its shell in the past 12 to 24 hours but is too hard to be considered "soft"

buster crab A crab that is in the first stage of shedding—its shell has just started cracking open

Chesapeake Bay The largest bay on the East Coast. Maryland and Virginia have many miles of shoreline on the Bay

culler a person who sorts crabs for the market

doubler A male crab connecting to and protecting a female who is about to shed

hard crab A mature male crab

jimmy A nickname for a mature male crab

peeler A crab that is about to shed its shell

rank crab A peeler that is just about to shed

sook A mature female crab

sponge crab An egg-bearing female crab

About the Author

Glenn Linton has been teaching art for more than thirty years. He grew up on Saxis Island, Virginia, a small fishing village on the Chesapeake Bay. During the early part of his teaching career, Glenn spent his summers crab potting. This book is an endeavor to share his love of art, teaching, and life on the Eastern Shore of Virginia with the child in each of us.

The story is presented through the eyes of Buster B. Bluecrab. Through Ole Buster, Glenn shares the experiences of life on the water in a fun and factual fashion. He gives a unique view of humans as seen from Buster's home beneath the water. Though Glenn now resides in Maryland, a part of him will always belong to his childhood home on the Bay.